THE PERFECT SCHOOL PICTURE

WRITTEN BY
DEBORAH DIESEN

PICTURES BY
DAN SANTAT

Abrams Books for Young Readers, New York

I'd planned for months.
This was going to be the year
of the perfect school picture.
But some days, not
everything goes
according to plan.

SEPTEMBER
SUNDAY
MONDAY
TUESDAY
WEDNESDAY
THURSDAY
FRIDAY
2
3
4
5
6
9
10
11
12
13
16
17
18
19
20
23
24
25
26
30

The day started with the worst case of bedhead *ever*.

Then it took me *quite* some time to unearth my favorite shirt. I finally found it at the *very* bottom of the hamper.

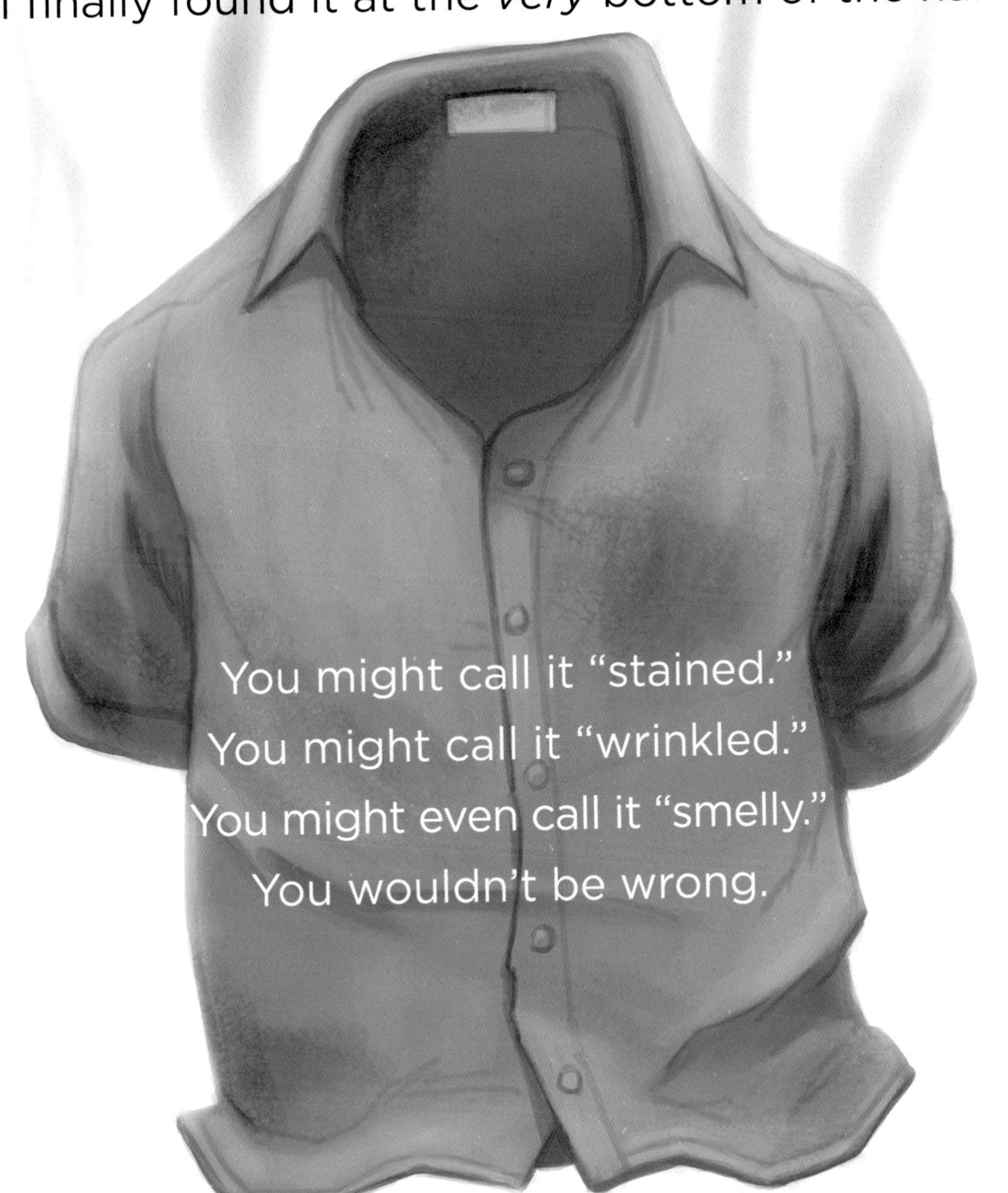

You might call it "stained."
You might call it "wrinkled."
You might even call it "smelly."
You wouldn't be wrong.

Breakfast was "Picture Day Pancakes," a family tradition. This year's festivities involved a small syrup disaster.

More accurately described as a *large* syrup disaster. And it occurred exactly as the bus pulled up.

I had a feeling we'd be getting a new family tradition.

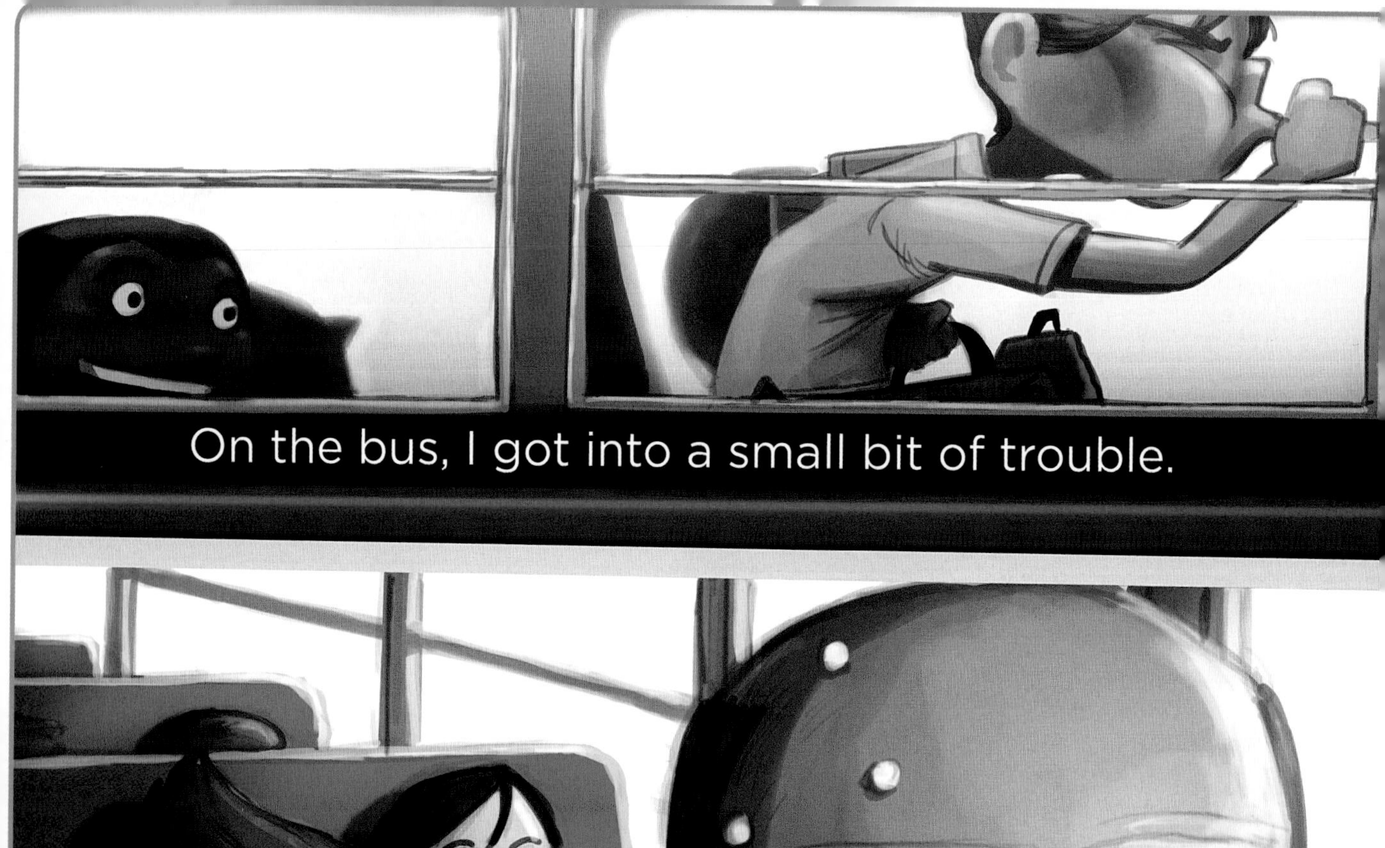

On the bus, I got into a small bit of trouble.

Make that a *large* bit of trouble.
The bus driver made me sit in the seat
right behind him for the rest of the ride.

By the time I got into school, my Picture Day face was fixed in a *scowl*.

In class, Mrs. Smith collected our photo order forms. Do you think my mom checked "Emerald Green" for my photo background? Or "Peacock Blue"? Or "Pizzazzy Purple"? No. Once again, of all the backgrounds in the world, Mom checked snoring-boring "Traditional Gray."
A B C D
T K
No one gets "Traditional Gray."
BACKGROUND COLOR
CHOOSE ONE:

Except for me.

And it just so happens to be the only color in the world that makes my favorite shirt disappear. All but the stains and the wrinkles.

After that, the teacher had us all stand up and practice our Picture Day smiles. Personally, I thought we needed a little something to get us in the Picture Day mood.

Whoops!

Got myself in trouble.

Again.

Luckily, I got to rejoin the class in time for Art.
Art involved quite a lot of paint.
Or at least it did for *me*.
GLOO

Finally, it was time to line up for our photos.

Ned, just in front of me, got the *last* complimentary plastic comb.

I watched as classmate after classmate smiled for the camera. I got queasy listening to everyone say "Cheese."

I can't *stand* cheese.

The mere thought of it turns me green! *Deeply* green. And just as my face reached its most *awful* pea-green shade, it was . . . *my turn.*

I stepped forward.
I sat down on the stool.
It was hard as a rock
and cold as an iceberg.

"Just a sec," said the photographer
as he fiddled with the camera knobs.

As I sat and waited, everything that had happened rushed through my mind. The monstrous messes. The muddles and the mix-ups. The whole day, from the moment I'd rolled out of bed, had gone . . .

PERFECTLY!

Even better than planned! This year, I was finally going to have *the perfect school picture.*

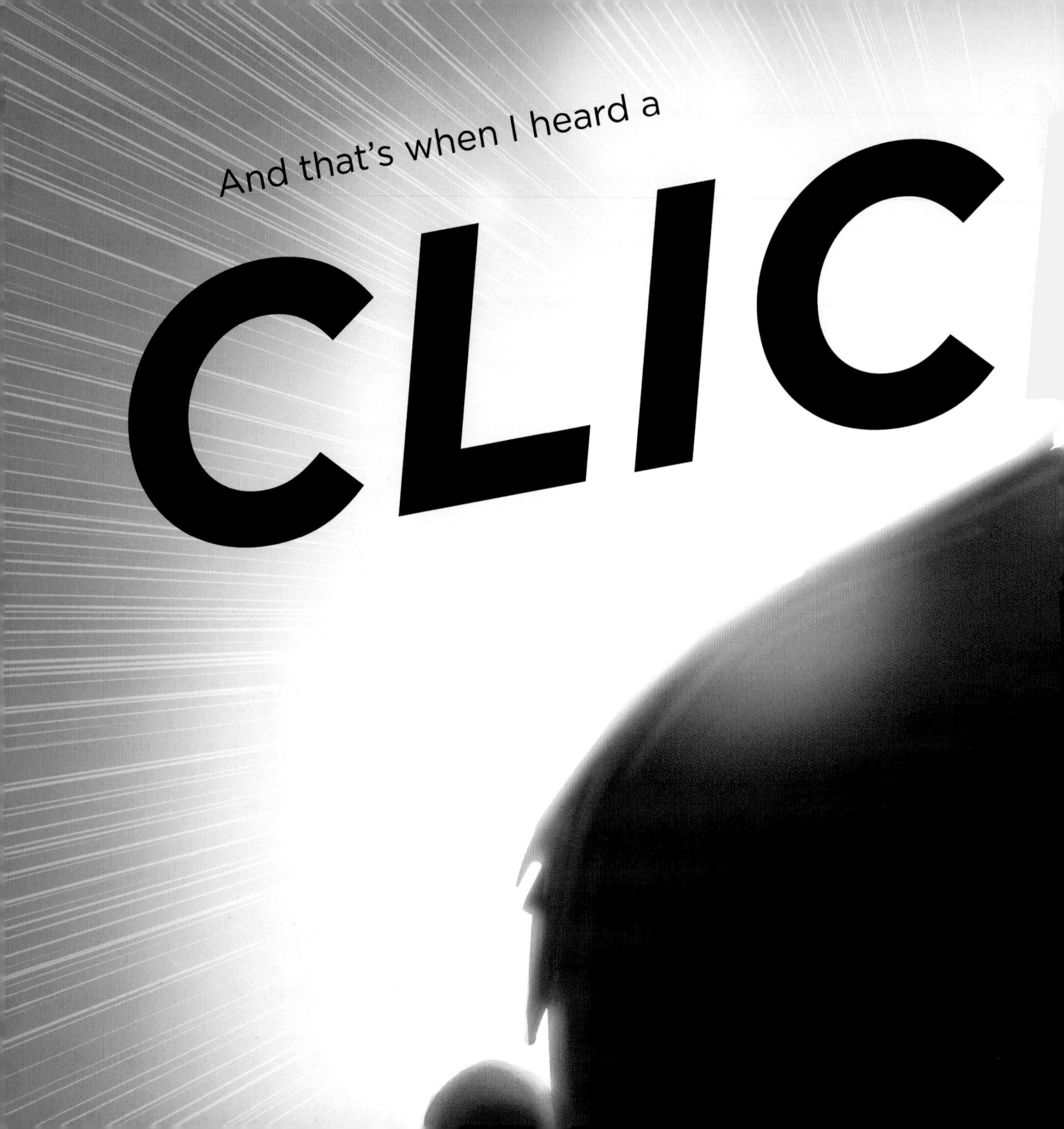

And that's when I heard a

CLIC

In a flash,
all my hard work—

my perfectly
tangled hair,
my perfectly
rumpled shirt,
my perfectly
sticky face,
my perfectly
composed scowl,
that perfect
boring background,
those perfect
paint splatters,
that perfect
sickly pallor—

WASTED!
USELESS!

RUINED**,**

in a moment of weakness,
by an unexpected smile.

Mom says it's my best
picture ever.

But just *wait* till she sees *next* year's.

24

PICTURE DAY

25

31

For my siblings, Tom and Ann
-D.D.

For Alek and Kyle
-D.S.

The Library of Congress has cataloged the hardcover edition as follows:
Diesen, Deborah. Picture day perfection / written by Deborah Diesen; pictures by Dan Santat. New York: Abrams Books for Young Readers, 2013.
1 v. (unpaged): col. ill.; 29 cm.
PZ7.D57342 Pic 2013
ISBN: 9781419708442

ISBN for this edition: 978-1-4197-3509-7

Book design by Chad W. Beckerman and Max Temescu

Originally published in 2013 under the title Picture Day Perfection by Abrams Books for Young Readers, an imprint of ABRAMS.

Printed and bound in China
10 9 8 7 6 5 4 3 2

Abrams Books for Young Readers are available at special discounts when purchased in quantity for premiums and promotions as well as fundraising or educational use. Special editions can also be created to specification. For details, contact specialsales@abramsbooks.com or the address below.

ABRAMS The Art of Books
195 Broadway, New York, NY 10007
abramsbooks.com